FIVE YEARS LATER
"Memoirs from a mother's diary"

COLLET HUNTER

FIVE YEARS LATER "Memoirs from a mother's diary"

COLLET HUNTER

DEDICATION

In the whole of my life, the greatest Joy I ever behold was the birth of my
sons, James Ross Hunter and Ryan Bowden Brodie Hunter. The love
bestowed throughout our journeys in this lifetime is priceless and cannot be
stolen. YES, I will forever hold on to joyful memories no matter what the
consequences are, you both have made it easy to love.

COLLET HUNTER

FIVE YEARS LATER "Memoirs from a mother's diary"

Foreword

We move to London 2009 he bonded with young, old, rich, poor and the homeless I would say persons from all walks of life. He was tutoring in school, teaching the young ones to dance his teacher told me after his death. He once said, "Mom not because someone does something bad makes them a bad person". Clothing, shoes, jackets were returned periodically as his friends did not have to wear to an event or party he once told me. I realized It was James journey to show passion strength, love and comfort to other. After speaking with those who knew him I was told I sound like him. This gave me comfort knowing he was loved as he once said to me. Friends still call from time to time and tell me stories of their dreams of him and feathers found. One said he was walking on the beach with a tiger as a pet brought a smile.

I recall from time to time our conversation when I told him I was going to lose him because of his love for others, he said "Mom I know you are right and I am prepared to face the consequences of my behavior". I left his room in silence and went into his brother room and told him James was on a special journey and he can leave us anytime; my son spoke about this for the first time in 2018 and asked how I knew. He told me he cried all night that night. . James was murdered weeks later as a peacemaker. James drew his own death we found it the day after the funeral from books his grandmother brought over from Jamaica. He mention the year five years later, the knife in the same hand the witness describe, the crowd that he intercepted, the mark on five boys in the crowd. (Five boys was charged) the figure of him punching in the group as described by the witness. Our many stories keep me going, the road where he was murdered we walked on it and I told him something was on there. Now I walk there without fear but with comfort and sometimes determination. Healing121 Community workshop is now a new venture.

True understanding of parenting skills and the loss of a child, it's a journey no one can prepare you for. Experiencing the beginning and ending of my nightmare and comfort. My journey of passion and growth with my two sons on their path to self-discovery was a milestone to achieve. No one could prepare me for losing my eldest James Ross Hunter just after he turned 18 years old to the waves of knife crime which still rock the city of London leaving trails of victims in grief. James died in his community saving another from a group of boys carrying knives. He bravely went in and save the boy who was kicking at the boys with knives he was already stabbed three times, James went over and punched them off him. JAMES ROSS HUNTER YOUTH SUPPORT A community organization has been set up in James memory as a legacy of peace. (Sunrise December 21, 1995 – Sunset May 31, 2014).The organization motto is "Encouraging Positive Social Values in Youths and Communities". A tree was planted in Wells Park where he played tennis and love to visit and also a garden set up on the spot he died with hope to bring solace and peace to those lives he touched here in London.

I wrote this book because of several factors. I realized James was special from an early stage. He was our miracle baby I was told I could not carry a child an injection was administered to aid with the birth process but this was interrupted by the tightening of the umbilical cord around his neck. I had to stop in the middle of giving birth to the medical team to cut the cord to release him, his grandmother held him as oxygen was administered. A series of events happened as he grew into a loving and caring child, one of our favorite was the bird with the broken wings that was found on the patio and was moved into the room as a pet and flew away on becoming stronger. This was truly a loving and tender memory of my sons together. I hope our many moments, conversations, poems, inspirations and passion shared in our lifetime will be of some value today. Love always,

Collet

COLLET HUNTER

Why So Long

What took us so long? Our children knew all along. Snitches, songs and baits. With care we share our passion and pain.

Yes, on our walk today. Women steps of dignity and unity. Tears did not flow. Link with arms and hearts aglow!
God lives within, this question always begin.

Why we waited so long to talk and support all along? Why oooooooh why?

I believe

I believe the hardest challenge is trying to show everyone everything is okay. With hope not to be judged because of loss but to cherish, accept, understand and heal with each memory bravely

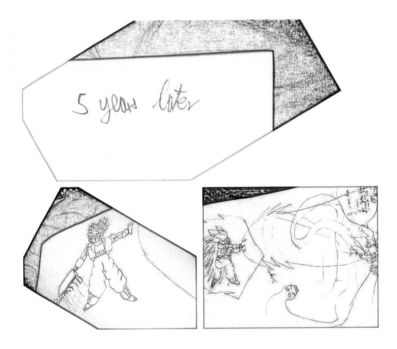

Pregnant

What to do, can this be true?

Have until noon is the results untrue?

Tests and test due to unrest, the possibility creates the best. What to do is this true?

The news now a little tune like a bubble of colors you form from doubles. So said the clouds, trees, stars and sea. A bundle of joy now God's creation.

Bouncing and kicking within with true emotions.

News

Our Joy began with great news.
News of birth,
Fresh as spring, gave us many reasons to sing.

The Christmas Present

Happy birthday!
Then came the morning without warning.
The angels open up to welcome cries so heartwarming,
The cord, oh the cord!
Oh so tight held you bawling but with great strength we welcome you
yawning.
Home Board!
Home board!
A package ever so priceless, our gift wrapped in all God's brightness!

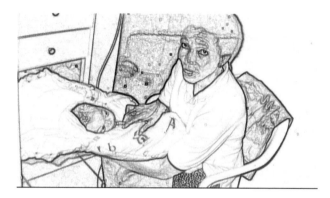

The Twos

The NOs and silly faces,
Sometimes filled with sea sandy salt taste,
Waddling feet standing, bonding, sitting balancing oh ever so priceless!
Unkempt hair in natural curliness,
Oh! Terrible twos sleepless and forever priceless!

Bee

So sweet, so special, chasing flowers.
Running around with swollen arm".
Stung by a bee, still has smiles of glee.
Petals flies in the wind, bringing rose, creating calm.
Little fingers on a journey that surely have begun.

Birds

When bird sings The sight so pretty, Feathers spoke and eyes went swollen, ooooh, looking hurts and now sooooo blurry. To the doctor we go, you are ever so cheerio!

Bird too

Can you spot the bird?

Broken wings, not able to sing.
In my room, nesting begins,
Cardboard boxes and Food to eat, oh boy what a treat!
Feeling better outside we go, up, up and away you go,
With wings to fly and places to go!

Kindergarten

Oh no, not there
Oh no, my dear
The gates shook and rattles,
I must not stay, around the block I go
Coming back to hear the cries of NO
Oh no I have to go so, we go, and we went to a place
Where there was no longer NO,
New school, filled with delights,
Fell in love with the very first site!

The Color Pink

Bouncing, playing, looking curly in dress, kicking ball with friends because of the mess! Care if you do or judge if you doubt, here is a boy running all about!

My Swagger

It was my time to go mom. No not to the prom. With thought of me
broken about what went wrong.
What ifs, what not? Judge me not. It was my time to go mom,
Remain strong.
I am here where I belong with angels making songs

School PTA

Deal of son, request and only one! Request brings reasons, sometimes
just one in each season!
The joy of knowing that present is care,
Peace in the making, Yes, life is very dear!

Think

Think twice, revisit when right, And when its bright!
"Now", yes the now can make or break you,
Can take you places that may erase you,
Comfort zone with no frowns,
Places that are known.
Think "no anger".

Anger

Moment spells, Hiccups of breaths,
Maddening pain in awe of nothing.
Throbs of visions and racing thoughts,
Again, taking many hearts.
With thoughts of you,
Stories unfold, testing all among the crowd!

Sunday Blues

In the beginning sounds old. A beautiful mind, say yes to folklores.
A beautiful action brings positive reaction.
Yes, Tennis racket back waiting!
Sun flowers opens up to the sun and kisses of blue skies,
Y E S another Sunday and gaming went by.

Love Steps

One, two, three,
A B C. Creep, Balance, Walk, Jump, Run, Skip.
Mistakes stones unroll, down came the books!
Tears of fright and surprise by mom!
Solid roots, unlock springs, hello rainbow storms.
Frighten by the falling books and save by love!

Grateful

Sip and taste without treasons.
To many reasons and sweet seasons,
Bellows at the moon and ponder with the sun,
The pleasure of hearts has begun,
Sounds of birds, breathless from love;
Thankful and gracious with stories from above.
Yes, my journey has just begun!

Rock

In the silence of doubts brings gleeful sounds.
It's comforting to look to the sky.
My yearly butterfly can't hide; through the storms you exhumed light in
tender moments.
Embracing messages of peace, love, forgiveness and hope to all folks.

Later

Every later is a story taker,
Yes, a message from the undertaker,
Yes, carry a cross so softly whispered.
A moment of comfort from life's creator.
A child taken and remade in God's grace, not forsaken.
Yes a child so precious. A child so dear.
A child born with nothing to fear.

Control

Control what if,
Control what's not,
Birds for all seasons. An inner light ever so bright, an inner peace,
creating ease.
Yes, action wings, facial motions, sound of crows across the oceans!

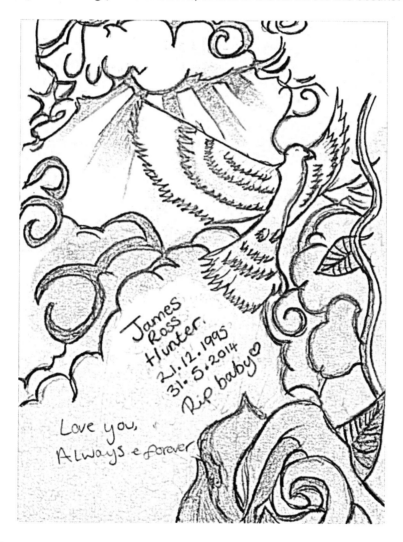

Trust

Trust an issue, cries will cry! Passion rise, doubt subsides. Those here and there feel the pain, knowing naivety brings sincerity,

Hello LOVE and prosperity.

Far

Away you climb,
Challenges and adventures combine!
Embracing the sun your journey has begun.
To the breeze, living your dreams
Whatever you please.
Now to the nest with stories so rest!
Here you bible creates no unrest.

COLLET HUNTER

Snow

Warmth of the sunrays so far "aglow"
Will it hurt?
How would I know?
Home at peace, making time for our feast.
My first snow, a reminder in every beginning.

Song

Oh, sweet song I know, so much sadness you sow.
Out of the song hummed sweet melody,
Yes, this I know, oh, sweet song,
You pick me up, when I am soooo low!
This is that time, oh yes I know

Stranger

Easy to smile A conversation so incline,
Drop pieces with various paces.
Where will it lead? This conversation with glee,
Bliss and joy now retreated
Facing another may bring doubt
Thoughts of you will always be about!

A Mothers Hug

A mother's love stems from above,
A healing moment, an abundance of love.
A mother's hug, so tender shared comfort from above.
A mother's hugs, this cannot be undone, many stories under the sun.
It runs over the hills through valleys,   echoing through every ally.
A mother's love,
Do exist in every hugs.

London Arrival

It sparks adventure, it brought hope, it came with sunshine grace and passion.
It was a new beginning of? What lays ahead it's the best for us, no doubts of pain.
Hello London, from afar you look like a giant of tender mercies.   Up close what makes you any different?

Hello London I'm here with all to gain? "Will the snow hurts"?
I tremble in its awe. It's my first snow I must remain calm.

Hello London, I'm open up to you. I taste the snow flake and breathe in ice cold brave with anticipation.

Hello London.

Teddy Dream

On the stretcher you lay,
We heard the news and came by,
Nerves flashing and eyes agape we wonder if it was too late,
Heard the news and saw it was true,
Here we both came looking for truth, then at a glance you smiled and it
all became clear as you turned into a teddy bear.

Feet

Kick, pull, stamp, twist, and punch you turned, YES!!
O what joy unfolded alive in my tummy!
YES in our world. Just when I thought I can't have anything to eat off
you silently went off to sleep.
Is it true? Can this be real?
We now have our own babies to keep.

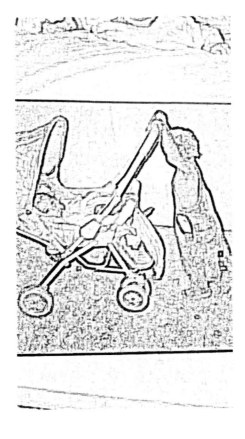

Happy Birthday

Happy is the day, happy is the moment it's never a time to forget it's
your birthday how can we forget?
The date is always our date a day we would always celebrate and never
late as its one we would always relate.
Happy birthday it will never ever be too late,
Still we celebrate.

Feathers

With hands open to make a call, you fall right into my palm.
With thoughts open to call a friend, you appeared with your feathery
calm, Peace and transparency, from the sky you fall.
In the midst of the crowd you choose my moment,
Out of the blue you sooth my mood,
Dear feathers you wave when my tides are low.
Keep on waving when I'm feeling low.

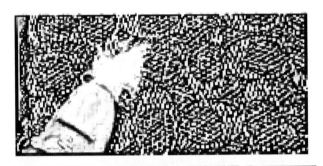

Granddad

Favorite memory with laughter your tooth fell out!! Granddad your
memory will live happily ever after,
You always find reasons in our conversations like many seasons.
Granddad you have sparked my journeys as you are never in a hurry.

Reindeer

First Christmas dear as a reindeer
Wearing horns and smiles, bobbing and bouncing like a rat,

Horns beckoning to life on another Christmas
Called "forget- me- not".

Looking out

You said you would not return,
Looking about brings back memory on this day.
I won't be coming back, Grandma remembers this day,
She did not understand but prayed.
I won't be coming back,
So you knew all along?

Sunrise

I look to each for comfort and hope.
The magical break away of the clouds offers new birth elevating my soul
to new highness,
Anticipation speaks volumes of bliss in every new day,
Flow to life here above and beyond the sun.

Send off

Today was your send off,
It was a day we knew was coming
However so soon was not our calling!
With arms outreach and hearts in tatters we gave our best holding our
heads together.
Today was the day to say goodbye "not forever,"

you will remain our treasures next to never.

The Tree

Planted then bless by our priest, with stories of peace to share.
Tarnishing doubts that covers cross roads,
Battling with symbols of who we are and what to become.
A tree planted with hope, strength, clarity and stamina.
Changes leaves, spring of new growth in this our smiles today.

Beach Bum

Forever a beach bum I will be,
A friend shared this dream of me, walking on the beach with a tiger as
my pet.
Forever a beach bum I will be,
Look at me still grazing in the sun

Passport

My very first passports don't get me wrong,
They said to sit still and smiles can't be long.
My first passport tells a tale of how you and I once hail and never fails.

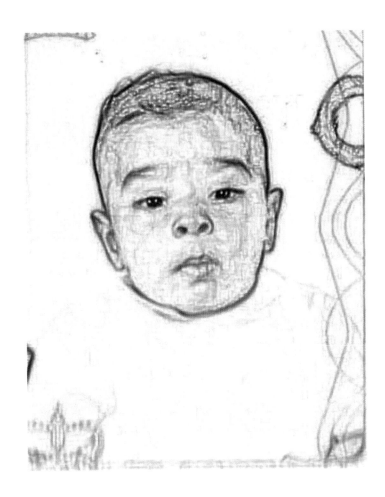

Hands

These hands are your weapons.
Train with the discipline to win, whatever the outcome,
A better you will become.
Hands take you many places through many races.

The outcome making paces as your journey began.

Friends From Afar

The moment we met I will never forget,
Into the now you bring colors with dance a flow,
Friends like you will never forget all opportunities gave no regrets.
Friends from afar always know where you are.

Beaching Feet

Pitter! Patter! Rhythm of feet, making melodies to the beach.
A sunny day with no crowd or frown and every reason to be found,
smiles so wide cannot hide.

Pitter! Patter! Of feet still lingers in my heart.

Mothers Of Streets

Tunes with wept and kept memories, brings joy on this anniversary.
You know the beats of all hearts.
Rising, caring passion for those depart.
Your hand print and heartbeat will never sink.
As you gave us so much to think.

Mother of the streets you are such a treat that lies beneath.

Dolphin kisses

Treats and upheld kisses,
Another new day, embracing you beyond the rays.
Shared heartbeats under the sun.
My journey has just begun.
Velvety touch never too much,
Grateful, an honor, so gentle, no rush and missing my dolphin touch.

Here We Go

The reason to face the consequences of love stems from reasons of
reality, the here and now can only be understood by the nature of care
and feeling of insecurities.
Here we go being truthful in words and deeds;
here we go observing the care in the now, with stories untold.

The Cross

It's never too much to carry,
I carry so many; it's never too heavy,
The comfort to know it lies across my chest forever gives me rest.
This cross I carry in many places it never stops my paces.

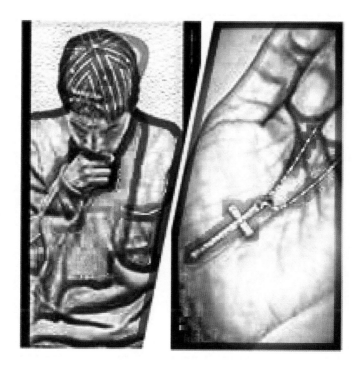

Father

Each birth begins with a father; it would not exist without one.
A father that supports and encourage.
A father who remain there with care.
No matter the sorrows life brings,

There are no seedlings without a father. Horsing around on a journey which has just began.

Vision one

Around a table you appear, with an angel with no fear,
You share your journey of below of all the friendship you sow.
All eyes bestowed with passion your explanation and earthly debate

I bravely visit the site of your light on the lane,
comforted from your story above.

Lunch

Can this be true? I received the news before I saw you.
With camera in gear so grateful to have you near.
I see no evidence of fear. Injured with evidence of blood, yet you were
so strong and said your friend did no wrong.
He was just hungry it was not intentional.

I realized where you belong and that you knew all along.

Dance

I heard your song today and dance,   with tenderness in a trance.
I remember those legs moving to the beat,
Beautiful thoughts that ever so sweet.
The timely rhyme you bring, not in a hurry to sing,
Looking so neat and ever so sweet,

Memories of dance moves that can't repeat,
Locked in our hearts forever as a treat.

A White Day

Can this be a dream? It all seems so unreal,
Within hours life is shaken like a leaf,
All with the changing of the weather.
Can this be true?

Even if it's a few snowflakes to keep me awake,
We cannot debate that the spring of a weather is never too late.

Miles

Across the waters and into my heart we were never a part,
it took this pain to bring us near not to tear our souls apart.
We took the challenge and accept the knowledge of deeper courage.
I am grateful for another moment and the magnet of love in my life.
My friend, my soul mate is this too late?

PASSION ONE

Think more than twice,

Create many thoughts with opportunities to revisits,

Situations remixes,

YES, another time,

When the time is right can be sure delight!

PASSION TWO

Everything you do or say in the "NOW" can be an icebreaker

"Now" not

later!

PASSION THREE

Anger should be the last resort because it's always the first to manifest!

PASSION FOUR

Give your Dreams wings of will and reality.

PASSION FIVE

Growth brings positive attributes with all things related to you.

PASSION SIX

Unlock your positive box each day. There is always something that connects with your journey.

PASSION SEVEN

Create rainbow reminders in your storms. Not necessarily has to be the place where you were born.

PASSION EIGHT

Make time. Time doesn't wait, it creates.

PASSION NINE

When in doubt, Embrace "you" and your beautiful spirit. Be grateful for you. The world will heal itself.

PASSION TEN

Hold on to smiles, be your own cheerleader.

PASSION ELEVEN

Glances at your surroundings will manifest something to be grateful for. Hold on to memories.

PASSION TWELVE

Use silence and doubtful moments for reflections.

PASSION THIRTEEN

A solid foundation matters. It withstands life's tremors, created earlier the better.

PASSION FOURTEEN

A latter foundation that's solid gives hope, strength and growth.

PASSION FIFTEEN

A positive foundation that held me together anytime my world seems to shatters.

PASSION SIXTEEN

Accept what is beyond your control and grow with every opportunities.

PASSION SEVENTEEN

Reach within and share, goodness... anything that's beautiful
will always glow.

PASSION EIGHTEEN

A tree understand the changes in the weather and spring the necessary leaves accordingly...I believe such is our lives.

PASSION NINETEEN

I believe we are measured by the company we keep, the memories that repeats and the passion underneath.

PASSION TWENTY

Never worry about those who wish you failure its the only
comfort they know, rise always with prayers.

PASSION TWENTYONE

The very best treatment you expect give it to yourself.

PASSION TWENTY TWO

What you feel is always real...it's your feelings!

PASSION- TWENTY THREE

I believe choosing friends involves insecurities of who and whats.

PASSION-TWENTY FOUR

The most fascination thing about failures? Its the oppotunities it brings
to try again...to make "YOU" right.

PASSION-TWENTY FIVE

Never let your past ruin your moment.

PASSION-TWENTY SIX

I believe our minds are like waves...continous in motions with many tales to tell.

PASSION-TWENTY SEVEN

No need to prove who you are. Just do it, continue to be "YOU" and stay in tune.

PASSION-TWENTY EIGHT

We all share one world, some through different version of views.

PASSION-TWENTY NINE

Uncountable waves on different journey and tides, all lives and stories as life journey continues.

PASSION-THIRTY

Find a spot and outshine yourself.

PASSION-THIRTY ONE

The sun never change only the clouds surrounding it.

PASSION-THIRTY TWO

Some tests are passed lessons, repeating itself for understanding and clarity.

PASSION-THIRTY THREE

On the discovery of your passion, rise each day with a dream, then
make it a reality. Treat it as your mission.

PASSION-THIRTY-FOUR

The memory of sound and laughter exist in silence, giving opportunities for individual growth.

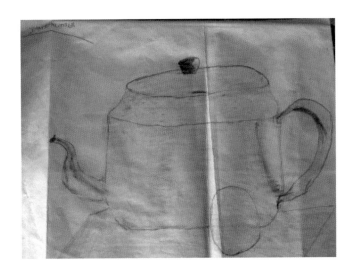

PASSION-THIRTY FIVE

You cannot compare sunsets. We are all beautiful and unique.

PASSION-THIRTY-SIX

Nothing fancy about simplicities.

PASSION-THIRTY SEVEN

Some will say that's a great idea and work with you. Some will say
that's a great idea and turn away, its about you living your
dreams...something no one can do for you.

PASSION-THIRTY EIGHT

Stay centered. Stay focus, it takes you plus your passion for growth,
not the thoughts of others.

PASSION-THIRTY NINE

Aim for floral thoughts.

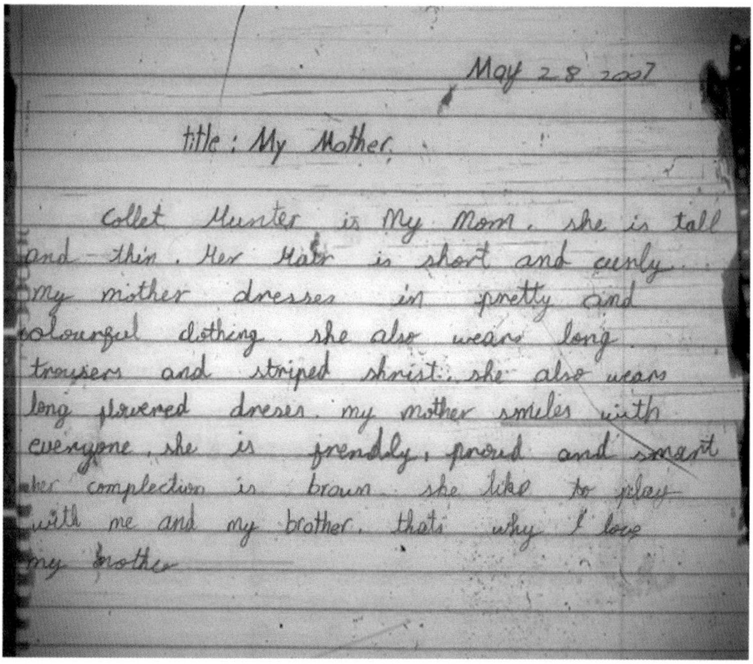

May 28 2007

title: My Mother

Collet Hunter is My Mom. she is tall and thin. Her Hair is short and curly. my mother dresses in pretty and colourful clothing. she also wears long trousers and striped shrist. she also wears long flowered dreses. my mother smiles with everyone. she is frendly, proud and smart her complection is brown. she like to play with me and my brother. thats why I love my mother

PASSION-FORTY

Break away, wise up. Yes, from anything negative.

PASSION - FORTY ONE

Not everyone like a survivor.

PASSION FORTY-TWO

The universe should not be questioned. It should be understood...this takes knowledge and positive awareness.

PASSION FORTY-THREE

Life is about valuing your existence not about riches, but about caring and sharing in the most humble ways possible.

PASSION – FORTY FOUR

We are all specks of dust passing through; I believe it's our hearts that determines our true values.

PASSION – FORTY FIVE

Forgetfulness sometimes brings comfort.

PASSION – FORTY SIX

Reminders and laughter brings memories.

PASSION – FORTY SEVEN

Anywhere you go passion and thoughts follows just like the sun rays.

PASSION – FORTY EIGHT

Joy will carry you when fates hits.

PASSION – FORTY NINE

If you smile at the world it brings peace. Complications begin with the choice to hate.

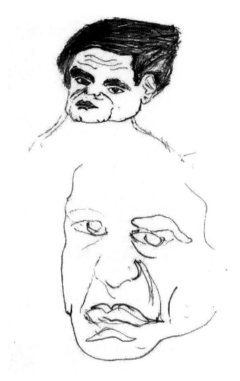

PASSION-FIFTY

No matter your views. Times, a season does not wait for anyone.

PASSION-FIFTY ONE

I believe our hearts are like closets...opening up shows our true values.

PASSION-FIFTY TWO

Like most things gratefulness is a part of self-awareness. The holy bible brings comfort.

PASSION-FIFTY THREE

Happiness is the power to be and stay happy in all that you say and do.

PASSION-FIFTY FOUR

When we embrace each other positive light, the world becomes a brighter place.

PASSION-FIFTY FIVE

I believe the transformation of a butterfly is proof from the universe
that true beauty comes from within.

PASSION-FIFTY SIX

The peace you gain is the peace you give.

PASSION-FIFTY SEVEN

I believe disappointments are reflections for the next appointment on a journey.

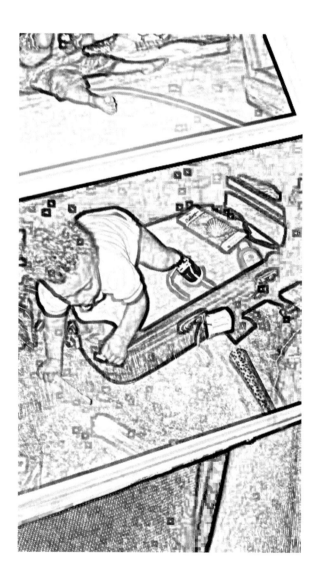

PASSION-FIFTY EIGHT

If your heart is at peace comfort will find you.

PASSION-FIFTY NINE

Nothing more to give? Give a smile.

PASSION-SIXTY

Be gentle, some spirits are easily broken.

PASSION- SISTY ONE

I believe we should aim to love, laugh and enhance each other.

PASSION-SIXTY TWO

Tick tock, the sound of the clock, it's the butterfly called "Forgetmenot"
Tick tock to bed I go with memories of "Forgetyou not"!

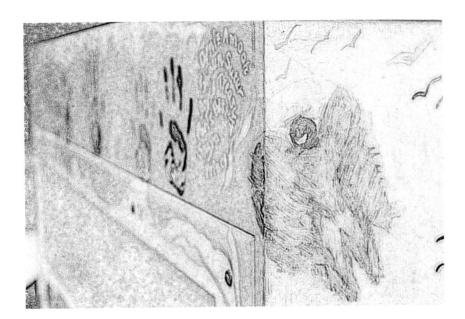

PASSION-SIXTY THREE

Something is wrong for not to show your feelings while balancing inner strengths.

PASSION-SIXTY FOUR

I believe it takes a vision of care to change a negative culture.

PASSION-SIXTY FIVE

It takes passion, courage, clarity, peace, love and understanding to replenish a great loss.

PASSION-SIXTY SIX

I believe the blissful joy you feel is a sell deserve treasure...

PASSION-SIXTY SEVEN

I believe your reflection and passion is you, creating a beginning in every endings.

PASSION-SIXTY EIGHT

The simplest pleasure is loving in every moment.

PASSION-SIXTY NINE

I believe we grow each time we lift each other up.

PASSION-SEVENTY

Healing is like a pulled muscle. It's consistent, return unexpectedly.
Good day and bad days.

PASSION-SEVENTY ONE

Rest you head on another...listen to a heart beat. That's how special we are.

PASSION-SEVENTY TWO

The moment you decide your spirit will not die, its a new beginning all over again.

PASSION-SEVENTY THREE

Listen to your heartbeat it tells your destiny, to embrace or recreate.

PASSION-SEVENTY FOUR

Bestow peace in all that you say and do. Heavenly wings today.
I believe heroes are selfless people who do what to be done, when it
needs to be done.
Blessed are the peacemakers they shall be called the children of God.
"Prayer of comfort Matthew 5:9"

PASSION-SEVENTY FIVE

Stay strong work on the inner you. Perfection will always be a battle.

PASSION-SEVENTY SIX

Be brave to love expecting nothing in return. A reminder of God healing grace and comfort.   Psalm 35 carried me through it all, the loss of my son.

PASSION-SEVENTY SEVEN

I believe the courage and the will to survive lies within.

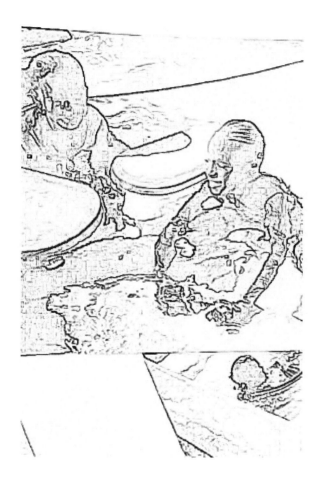

PASSION-SEVENTY EIGHT

Worrying about a broken wing should not stop the hope from flying once again.

PASSION-SEVENTY NINE

I believe the universe and you equal dreams and destiny.

PASSION-EIGHTY

Start with a good mind and the rest will follow.

PASSION-EIGHTY ONE

Life is like a bag, without the handles you may lose the grip, holding on matters in all circumstances.

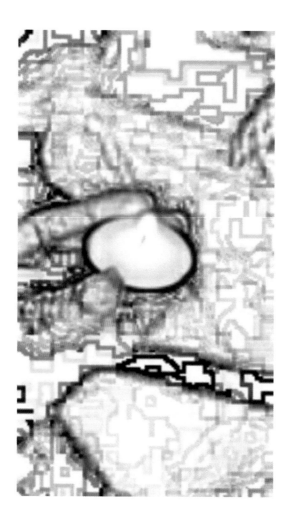

PASSION-EIGHTY TWO

My definition of peace is where answers are given in silence.

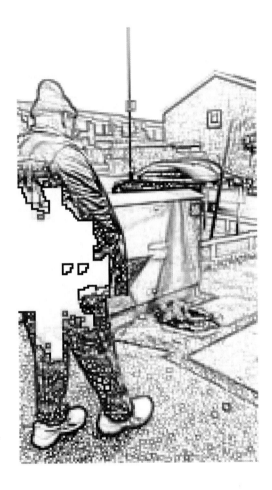

PASSION-EIGHTY THREE

The most valuable things we have are each other.

PASSION-EIGHTY FOUR

Fears are like hidden tears, lerking to happen.

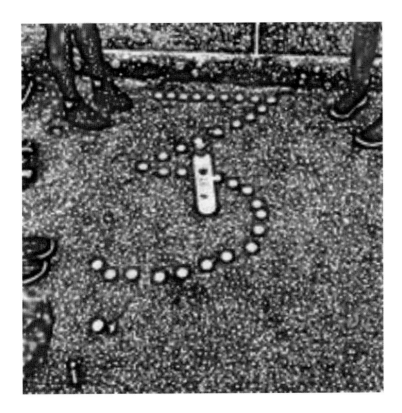

PASSION-EIGHTY FIVE

Focus on your future; no one can change the past.

There is a time
to mourn,
cry and pray
no time for hate
...on life journey

PASSION-EIGHTY SIX

You always have the power and the choices to bring out the best in you.

PASSION-EIGHTY SEVEN

Your thought does not become you. It's your actions.

The power of knowing and growing. The difference between day and night is the time, and the light.

PASSION EIGHTY EIGHT

Lives make sense if we all love, care and share.

PASSION-EIGHTY NINE

A star does not compare with the star next to it, but shine on even falling leaving trails of memories that lives on.

PASSION-NINTY

A friend who comes to stay will continue to walk with you in everyway.

PASSION-NINTY ONE

The most beautiful experience is a beautiful soul.

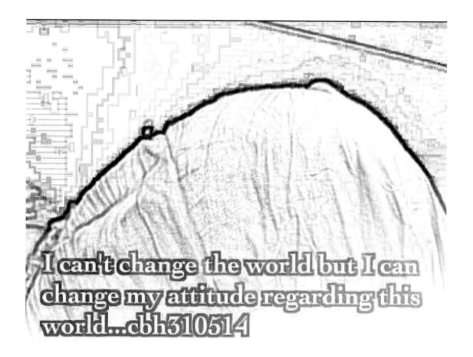

PASSION-NINTY TWO

When dreams are broken go back to the beginning.

PASSION-NINTY THREE

It takes you to discover you. Not the crowd.

PASSION-NINTY FOUR

It takes one moment to bring regrets.

PASSION-NINTY FIVE

I believe if you don't make room for understanding the tears of fears will forever be "criss-cross".

PASSION-NINTY SIX

It's so easy to break a pace without a pacemaker, all things and actions stems from a foundation of care.

COLLET HUNTER

PASSION-NINTY SEVEN

The air for misunderstanding always lingers.

PASSION-NINTY EIGHT

The rise and fall of passion depends on WHAT motivates. "YOU".

PASSION-NINTY NINE

People will always come and go appreciate the effort, place and time.

PASSION-ONE HUNDRED

I believe one of the most beautiful gifts given is love.   No matter how many times taken. Love well.   Live well.   Spread wealth.   Be at peace.

Acknowledgments

To the many thousands of people who have purchased "Daisy Pins" displaying support for victims and sharing visual awareness to violence and knife crime.

 To the organizations that supported James Ross Hunter Youth Support events and projects in London, since July 2014.

 To the people who have given their time to contribute, volunteer and support JRHYS community events and projects, and hear me speak of James legacy of peace.

 To the many who have sent email, cards and made contact with me. This has humbled me on this journey.

 To the many that still reach out with comforting words and support each moment helped.

 To: my close friends, family members, my mother Valrie and Son Ryan who continues to inspire me daily. To all the positive energies that come my way from all of you my friends.

God bless, as life journey continues.

FIVE YEARS LATER "Memoirs from a mother's diary"

Printed in Great Britain
by Amazon

57876249R00091